16-296R

16-296R

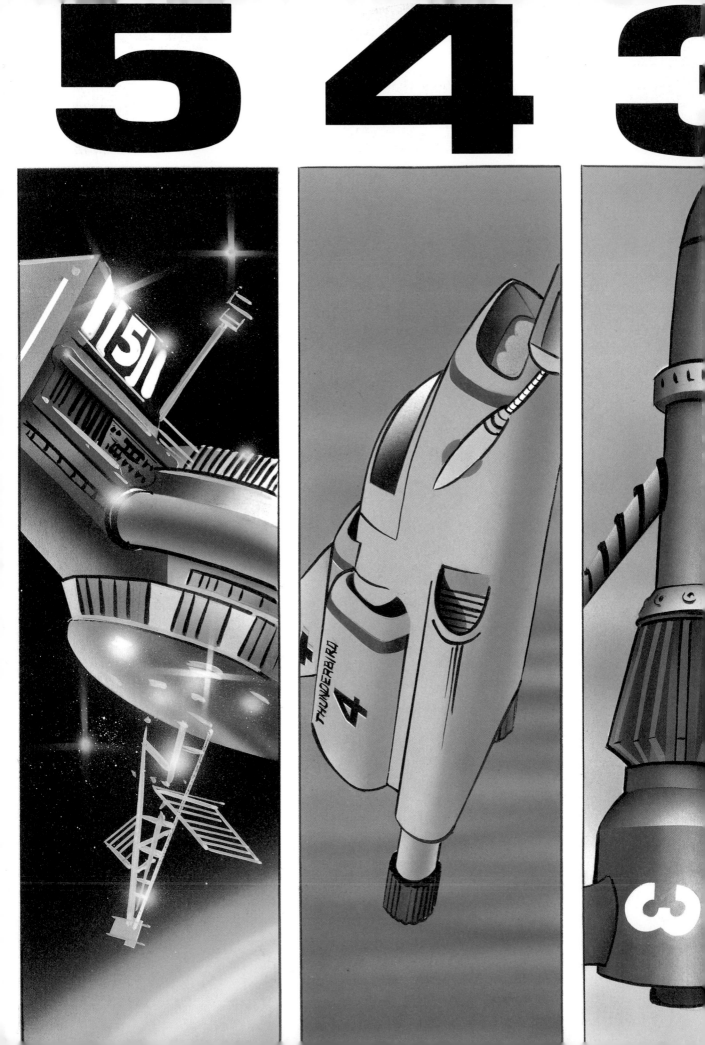

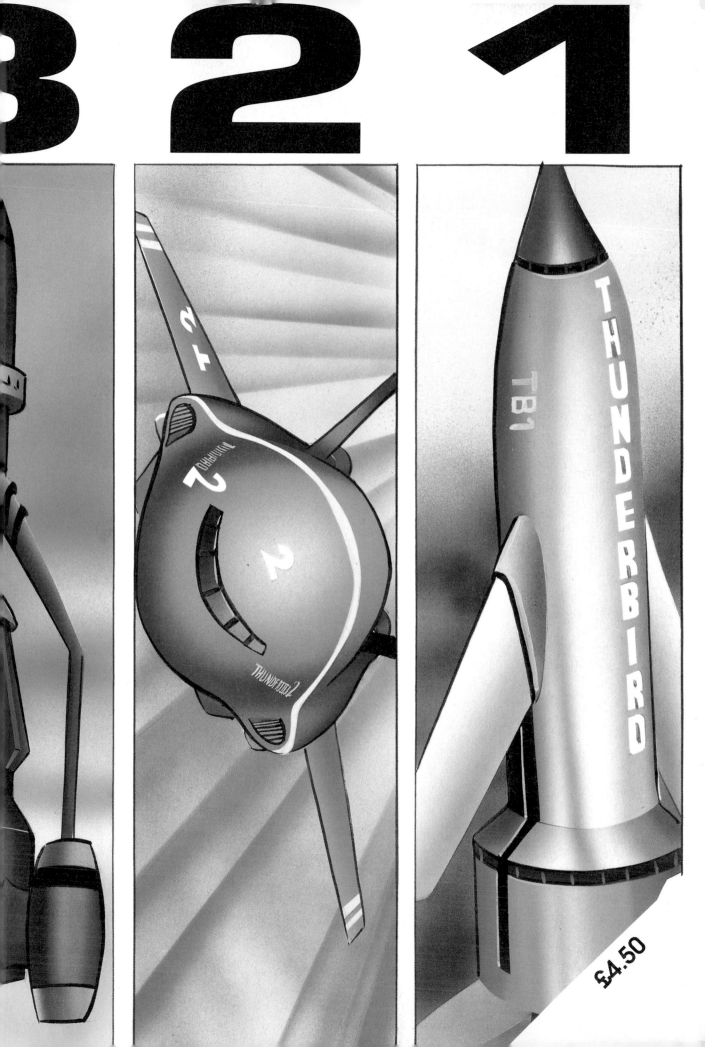

Published by

Grandreams Limited,
Jadwin House,
205/211 Kentish Town Road,
London, NW5 2JU.

Printed in Belgium.

ISBN 0 86227 953 4

THUNDERBIRDS ARE GO

THE INTERNATIONAL RESCUE YEARS

1970

1990

1992 Jeff begins astronaut training

1996 Scott born

1997 Jeff develops theories on

1998

1999

2000 Jeff chosen to commemorate 21st

2001 Jeff wins contract to build shuttle and other space hardware

2002-15

2004 Gordon born

2005 Alan born - Lucille dies.

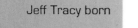

Jeff Tracy born

Jeff joins U.S. Air Force

Jeff marries Lucille
and makes Grandma very proud

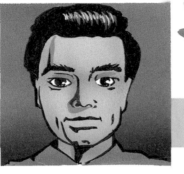

Sun's rays as a power
boost for rockets

Jeff looks at
new metals

Jeff transferred to newly formed World Space Agency.
Allowed to set up small business - space hardware construction. Virgil born

century with special Moon mission

John and
Brains born

Tracy Construction and Aerospace companies developed

University of Kansas honours Jeff by naming   a college after him

Astronaut training
at Tracy College

Scott to complete
astronaut training

Virgil begins astronaut training after graduating from the

Gordon becomes an aquanaut with World Aquanaut Security Patrol (WASPs)
Jeff involved in sinking liner disaster

Jeff is victim of mutiny. He is presumed lost in Pacific

Jeff to set up International Rescue.

Alan becomes an astronaut.   Jeff secures contract to build a space station.

Thunderbird 5 completed

International Rescue's first mission

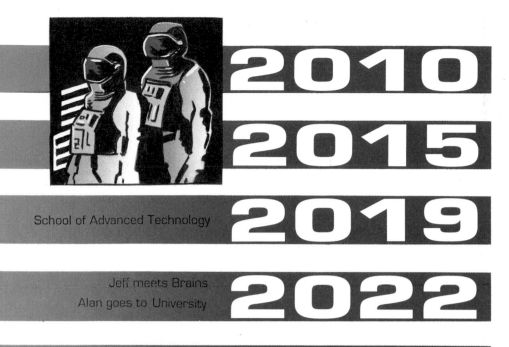

2010

2015

2019

School of Advanced Technology

2022

Jeff meets Brains
Alan goes to University

John goes to Tracy College to become an astronaut
Jeff has breakdown - advised to relax - decides to travel

Jeff in private plane crash in Malaysian jungle
Jeff meets Kyrano and Tin Tin

2023

Scott and Gordon find Jeff   Jeff meets Brains again - in Paris

Intense activity as Thunderbirds 1,2,3 and 4 are constructed

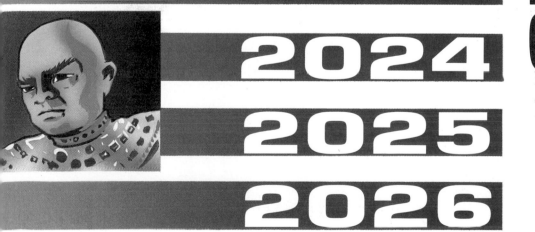

2024

2025

2026

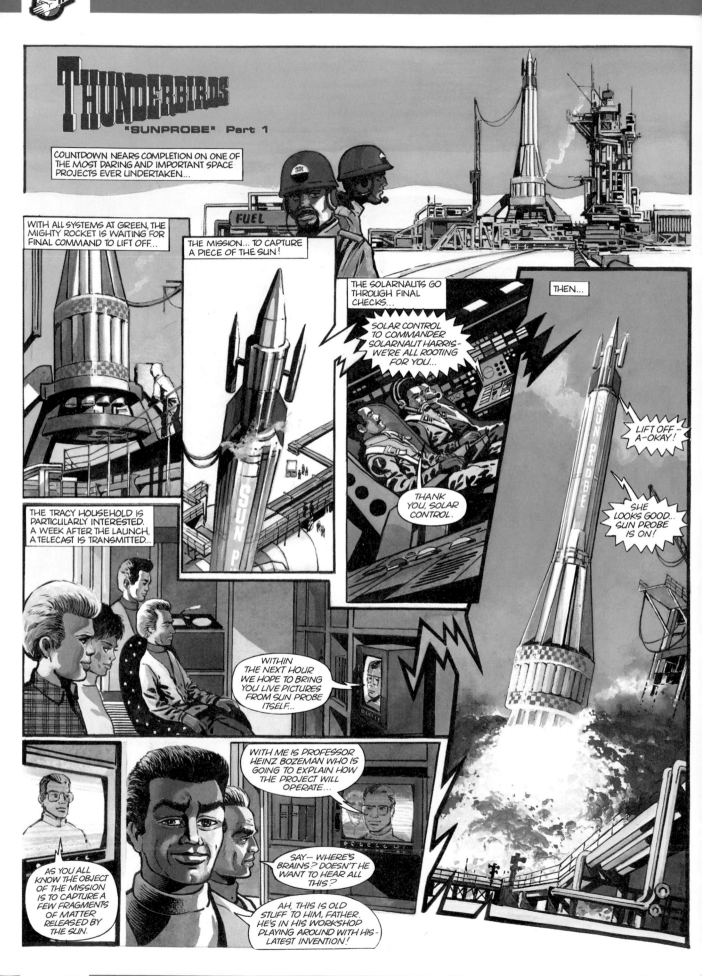

CONTINUED ON PAGE 28

The founder of International Rescue, Jeff Tracy started life on a Kansas wheat farm. His father was combine harvest driver and this mechanical vocation possibly influenced young Jeff to become interested in machinery.

His military service was spent with the U.S. Air Force, and from the ranks he rose to a colonel before transferring to Space Agency projects.

He was an instant success as an astronaut and has the distinction of being chosen for the Moon flight that celebrated the arrival of the twenty-first century.

Jeff built a highly profitable company manufacturing and developing shuttles and space related hardware. He went into civil and construction engineering and became, in a short time, one of the richest men in the world.

Then tragedy struck the Tracy household. His wife Lucille, died prematurely and the raising of five robust and healthy sons became Jeff's first duty.

After a difficult period, Jeff turned his attention to people less fortunate than himself and he conceived the idea of International Rescue. From his plans and spirit of enterprise, the organisation took shape and became a reality.

Jeff is intelligent, kindly and has a sense of humour but when the situation demands, he can be decisive and occasionally very stern.

Date of birth: January 2nd

Not one of the Tracy family, Brains is none-the-less one of the most important people in the International Rescue team.

He has brain power and inventive genius beyond his years and is the mastermind behind many of the wonder machines used by the organisation.

Very serious, he is rarely satisfied with what he produces and is constantly working on modifications to his creations.

Brains' hobbies include higher mathematics and the pursuit of perfecting a robot named Braman which he developed primarily as a chess adversary. Brains is currently translating Einstein's Theory of Relativity into computer speak.

Orphaned when a hurricane struck his Michigan home, Brains was adopted at the age of twelve by a Cambridge University professor who recognised the boy's phenomenal ability to learn.

Jeff Tracy's contact with Brains followed after Jeff had conceived the idea of International Rescue. He realised that a super-mind would be needed to make the organisation a reality and he toured the world searching for a genius. Jeff's enquiries and questing led him to a small cultural hall in Paris, and Tracy realised instantly that Brains, who was nervously delivering a fantastic lecture, was the man to fulfil a dream. Brains accepted the challenge without hesitation. Real name Hiram J. Hackenbacker, Brains is twenty-five-years-old.

Date of birth: November 14th.

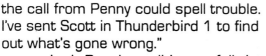

the call from Penny could spell trouble.
I've sent Scott in Thunderbird 1 to find
out what's gone wrong."

Lady Penelope slid gracefully into
the hide leather rear seat of Fab 1 as
Parker operated the gull-wing door.
"Thank you, Parker. Let's hope the
mobile radio can reach Tracy Island
without interference."

Before Penelope could operate
the radio, there was the rumble of an
explosion, and then, without warning, Fab
1 was tossed across the driveway of the
mansion, with Parker following like a
piece of wind-flung paper.

The Rolls Royce finished up on its
roof, with Lady Penelope inside, now
unconscious from striking her head on
the door frame.

When Scott arrived in
Thunderbird 1, he glanced at the scene
below at the front of the house. The
workmen were gathered around the
overturned Rolls Royce and an
ambulance, swiftly alerted by the
engineers, was in attendance.

"I'd better land away from the
house," Scott decided. "Don't want to
present those folk with any more
surprises."

Scott landed in the midst of a
copse of trees and, changing out of his
uniform to civilian clothes, he made his
way towards the mansion.

Lady Penelope was recovering
and Parker, holding his aching head,
looked bewildered. "We'll have to get you
to the hospital, your Ladyship,"
announced one of the ambulancemen.

Shaking her head in protest, Penelope was relieved to see Scott Tracy pushing his way through the small crowd. "Let him through," said Penny. "He's my personal doctor."

Scott blinked in surprise and then tried to learn what had happened.

"It was the digger again," said one of the engineers. "We went straight through the gas main...and a spark did the rest!"

"Swipe me!" exclaimed Parker. "When you go to town with that machine, you really have a smashing time, don't you?"

Scott took charge of the situation and helped her Ladyship back to the house, dismissing the others. Parker followed, still confused.

"I didn't know you were a doctor, Mr Scott," he said. "I keep getting this pain in my right toe...the big one. Do you think you could take a look at it..?"

"Oh, Parker," laughed Penny. "Scott is not a doctor. I only said he was so that we could get rid of the ambulancemen."

Once in the drawing room, Penelope quickly told Scott the reason for her attempted calls.

"So you see, Scott," she finished, "the missiles are targeted to land directly on Moratoa Island."

"Moratoa!" gasped Scott. "That's where International Rescue's auxiliary stores and fuel are based. If those missiles hit the island it will cause a tidal wave that will be felt all around the Pacific."

Making sure Penelope and Parker were sufficiently recovered, Scott returned to Thunderbird 1 and took off for the Pacific.

"Thunderbird 1 to International Rescue. Come in, father. This is vital!"

Jeff Tracy called Brains and Virgil to the control desk. "The missiles are due to be fired in less than two hours. What do you think, Brains?"

"Well, Mr Tracy," replied the brilliant mind behind many of the Thunderbird craft. "The Vanta-7 missile

is a normal remote-controlled weapon. It homes in on its target, controlled by radio and laser beams linked to a network of orbiting satellites."

"When it gets within the target area," added Virgil, "a robot camera eye system takes over for the final run-in."

Brains nodded grimly. "And believe me, Mr Tracy, once that robot lens has spotted Moratoa Island, there's no turning it off course."

Jeff pondered on the information. "So, the missiles cannot be intercepted, and once on course, there's very little we can do to stop them. And it's certainly no good appealing to that dictator Barach. He wouldn't care even if we revealed what was stored on Moratoa."

"And to explain that would mean blowing International Rescue's cover," said Virgil.

Brains suddenly drew in a deep breath. "Mr Tracy, the store of silver nitroglobe particles...what is the p-present strength?"

Jeff looked puzzled. "Two hundred tonnes, I guess, Brains. But the store is not on Moratoa - it's here, on Tracy Island."

"We use it to cool our atomic fuel supplies," Virgil reminded them.

MISSILE ALERT

"Exactly!" announced Brains. "This is what we h-have to do. L-load as much of the SNP as we can spare aboard Thunderbird 2. Then, Virgil, you must scatter the p-particles over the sea in the specific section that I will p-plot."

Jeff and Virgil looked at each other in puzzlement as Brains hurried towards his laboratory. "Well," said Jeff "You heard him, Virgil. Let's get on with it. Brains will let us in on his plan when he's ready."

Soon Thunderbird 2 was ready to be launched. Virgil took up his position in the control cabin, and minutes later, Brains joined him.

"Right, Virgil," Jeff's voice came over the radio.

"Thunderbird 2 is clear to go."

"We have j-just over an hour, Virgil," Brains said softly. "That's if President Barach has carried out his threat."

The cliff face opened and the mighty Thunderbird 2 taxied out of its cavernous hangar and rolled majestically towards the launch ramp. When the ramp had been raised, there was a deafening roar of its powerful engines, and then Thunderbird 2 moved slowly but surely into the air.

Virgil banked the great aircraft in a tight turn and headed for Moratoa Island. Exactly at the spot decided by Brains, the silver nitroglobe particles were released.

"Now all we can d-do is sit and wait," said Brains when the job was done. "Thunderbird 1 will be here soon. We'd better warn Scott that there could be some changes to his v-visual bearing marks."

Thunderbird 1 reached the area almost at the same time as the three Vanta-7 missiles. Two miles ahead of him, shimmering on a glass-like sea, Scott saw the silhouetted outline of Moratoa Island. Every detail, every rock and boulder stood out with stark clarity against the disc of the rising sun. And there was something else, too. At twenty thousand feet, three slivers of black were streaking through the sky.

"The Vantas!" Scott exclaimed. "There's nothing we can do. Guess Brains's plan, whatever it was, didn't work. Those missiles are bang on course and the robot camera-eyes are in operation. Nothing - no power on Earth - can stop them now."

Brains and Virgil, flying slowly around the area in Thunderbird 2 watched in fascination as the missiles suddenly took up a new course and swung down into a steep dive.

"It's w-working!" shouted Brains. "L-look, Virgil...they're d-diving. Plunging for their final run at the target!"

"Are you crazy?" Scott's voice came over the radio link. "The island and millions of dollars worth of essential supplies will be destroyed!"

Next second, the missiles were speeding low over the surface of the sea...and then they exploded in a devastating, eardrum-splitting, eyeball searing flash of destruction.

Scott's jaw fell, his lungs expelling a long gasp of air. The island had disappeared. Not a single trace of it remained.

Virgil smiled grimly at Brains as, moments later, Scott's voice filled Thunderbird 2's cabin. "Brains...was I seeing things? The island was there. I saw it! And then, just as those missiles plunged in, it disappeared!"

Brains nodded, a slow smile of relief spreading across his young face. "True...b-but that's because it was only a mirage...not the real thing!"

"A mirage!" gasped Scott. "You mean you actually created a mirage? An optical illusion for those robot camera eyes to home in on?"

"Y-yes," replied Brains over the radio. "You see, m-mirages occur when the air is very still and either very cold or very warm in its lowest part. The air settles into l-layers and the light is reflected from the surface of these layers as it passes through them. This reflection of l-light distorts it, and the image of distant objects - in this case M-Moratoa Island - is raised in the air, to become a mirage."

"So that's why Thunderbird 2 spread the load of ice-cold silver nitroglobe particles over this area," Scott realised. "By creating the mirage before the missiles reached the real island, you fooled those robot camera-eyes into detonating too soon."

"Exactly!" said Brains. "Now perhaps we can go home. I-I could do with some breakfast..."

Two hours later, Lady Penelope and Parker listened to a newscast. Owing to a change of plan, President Barach had decided not to launch the Vanta 7 missiles "to comply with the wishes of the World Council!"

"That man is a menace to world peace," Penelope said firmly. "Not only does he break treaties, but he tells an awful lot of lies."

Parker remained standing by the drawing room entrance. "Eh, those cowboy workmen 'ave finished making a mess of the countryside, M'Lady," he announced. "What are we going to do about the Rolls Royce. It's in a bit of a mess."

"Yes, Parker," replied her ladyship. "I'll have a word with Brains before we carry out the repairs. It is possible he will have some suggestions about effective modifications to improve Fab 1's performance and functions."

Lady Penelope prepared to make the call to Tracy Island. "Oh, Parker," she said, "you don't have to clean the car today."

"Yus, M'lady," Parker nodded and left Penelope to speak to Brains.

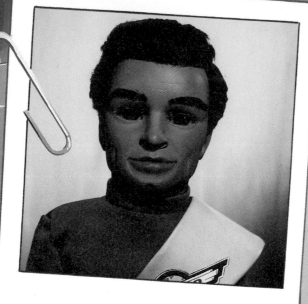

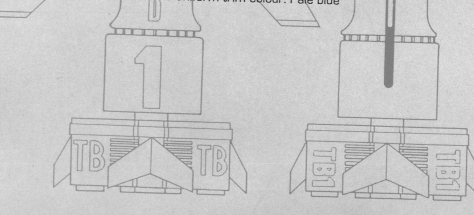

At thirty years of age, dark-haired Scott is the eldest of the Tracy boys. He was educated at Yale and Oxford Universities and during his term of service in the U.S. Air Force gained many decorations for valour and bravery.

His main job is to fly Thunderbird 1, International Rescue's reconnaissance aircraft, but his duties extend to control of the organisation whenever his father is absent from the island headquarters.

In addition, he invariably accompanies Alan Tracy as co-astronaut in Thunderbird 3.

There is much of his father in Scott's character - he is always ready to enjoy a joke and speaks in a short, decisive fashion.

Tremendously powerful in the physical sense, he is also extremely knowledgeable and wastes no time in making up his mind.

The responsibility of assessing a disaster situation and deciding which rescue craft to use, falls on Scott's shoulders because he is nearly always the first I-R man on the scene of a calamity.

With ceaseless energy, he manages to exist on very little sleep and is always light-hearted and full of vitality, seemingly without a care in the world.

Date of birth: April 14th   Sash and uniform trim colour: Pale blue

24

THUNDERBIRD TRIVIA QUIZ

How many questions can you answer?

1. Which of the Tracy brothers pilots Thunderbird 1?

2. The Hood has a hideout in the jungle. What type of building is it?

3. What is International Rescue's tunnelling machine called?

4. Who is I.R's London agent?

5. What is the name of the Thunderbird's space station?

6. Thunderbird 3 goes into space. Which craft goes under water?

7. What is Kyrano's daughter called?

8. Where is Tracy Island?

9. How many sons has Jeff Tracy?

10. What is the name of Lady Penelope's chauffeur?

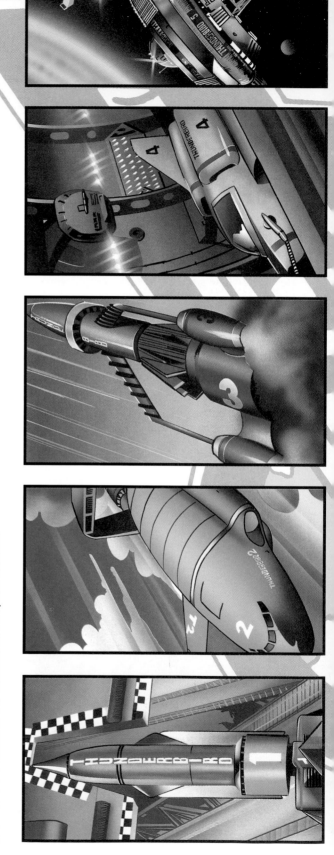

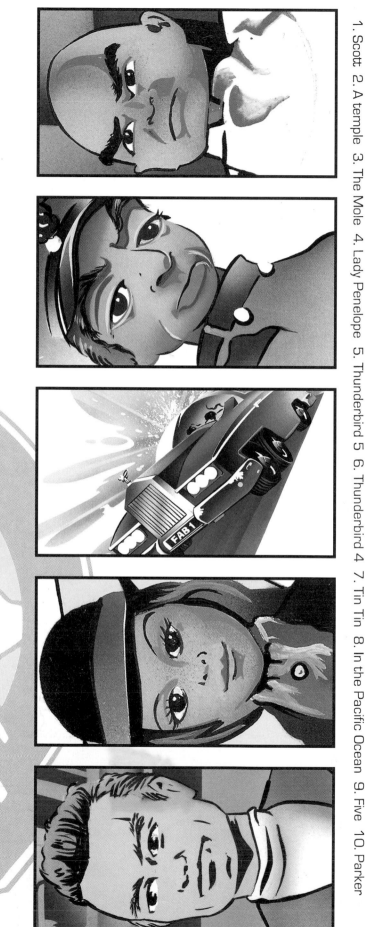

CROSSWORD

How quickly can you solve this puzzle?

Clues across:
1. TB1 pilot
5. Father Tracy
7. Make a meal
8. ... and bolt
9. Sugar lump
10. Motor
11. Striped animal
13. Pilot of TB3
16. Has had food
17. And ... to bed
18. Revolve

Clues down:
1. Red thing in the sky
2. Tenth month
3. Tom without the 'm'
4. Number one Moggie (two words)
6. I-R call sign
9. Bird with long legs
12. Hurried
14. Request
15. Not without the 't'

Answers:

Across: 1. Scott; 5. Jeff; 7. Cook; 8. Nut; 9. Cube; 10. Car; 11. Zebra; 13. Alan; 16. Eaten; 17. So; 18. Turn.

Down: 1. Sun; 2. October; 3. To; 4. Top cat; 6. FAB; 9. Crane; 12. Ran; 14. Ask; 15. No.

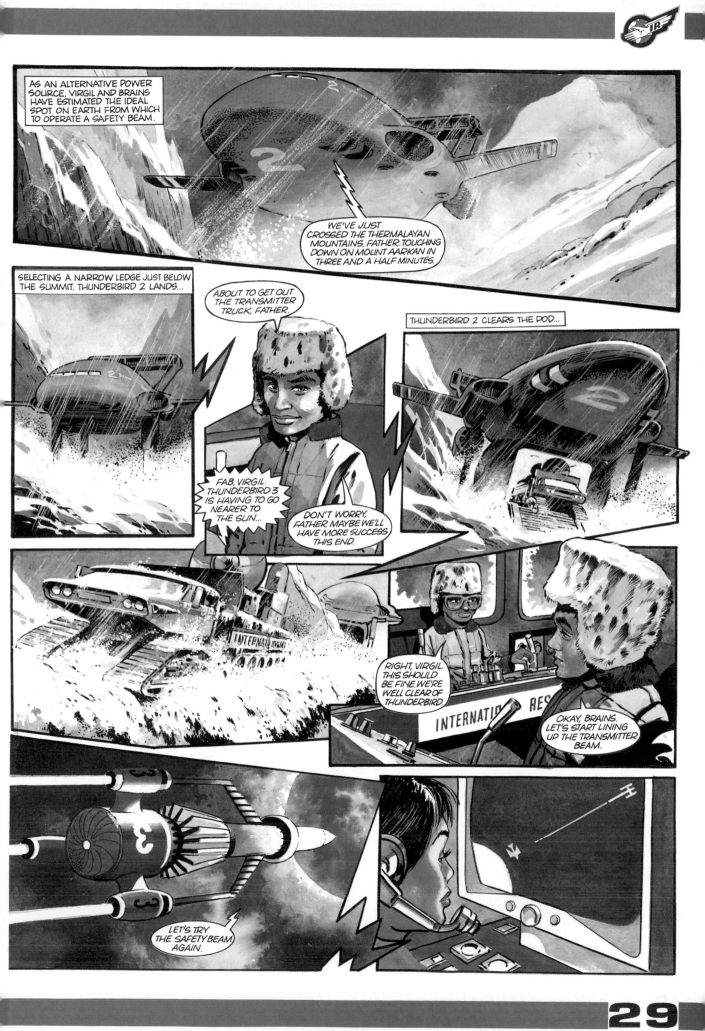

CONTINUED ON PAGE 50

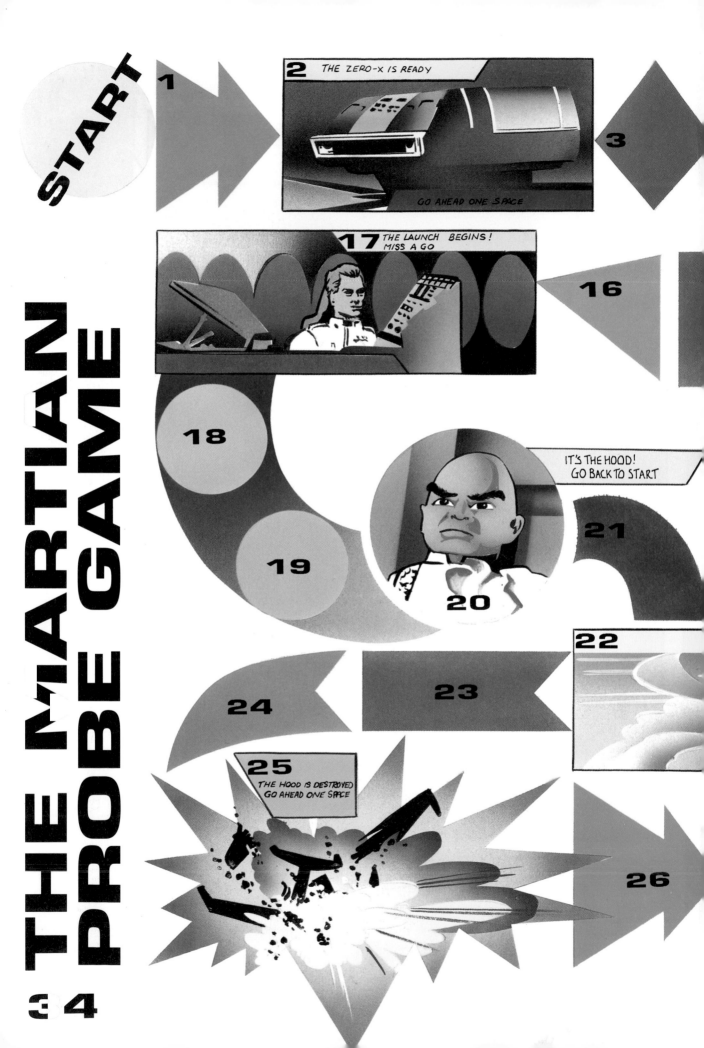

Baby-faced, blond and twenty-on[e,] Alan is the astronaut mainly responsible f[or] Thunderbird 3. Alan has been to the Moo[n] many times and, with his brother John, shares terms of monthly duty in Thunderbird 5, I-R's orbiting space station. He is the romantic of the family and likes nothing better than to explore the rocks and pot-holes located in the more inaccessible parts of Tracy Island.

But there is no romance in his attitude to the work of International Rescu[e.] He sees it as a vital service to mankind and is as dedicated as his father.

Alan has always had his eyes on the stars. This dedication does not prevent him from being a bit of a practical joker, and if any of the Tracy's could be termed reckless, it must be Alan.

From an early age he became interested in space travel and once built a rocket which went off course, shattering every window in Colorado University. His father decided after this incident that astronaut training was the only thing which would give Alan a sense of responsibility, and Jeff's decision was upheld by Alan's ability in space. A great sportsman, he is the life and soul of the party.

Date of birth: March 12th   Sash and trim colour: Off-white.

"Boy, am I glad to be handing over to you!" John Tracy slapped his brother Alan on the shoulder and grinned. "One month up here sure is enough."

The two men stood by the access ramp of International Rescue's space satellite, orbiting far above the Earth. Outside, the huge bulk of Thunderbird 3 lay locked in the communication position, waiting to take John back home after his routine spell of lonesome duty.

A final wave of his hand, and he walked through the automatic locks into the control cabin of Thunderbird 3. His hands sped over the controls with the ease of long practice, and the initial motors drew the massive craft slowly out of contact with the satellite.

At once, John opened long-range communication with the tropical island base where his father and the rest were waiting, and read over his atmosphere re-entry course. Then, at full boost, the space cruiser began its long haul home.

There were many sounds in Thunderbird 3 to break into John's thoughts on such a flight. Radio atmospherics, the ticking of the sensitive instruments of the control panel - but there was one sound more than usual. Too low to be noticed over the rest - low

like the first hiss a snake makes before a strike at an unsuspecting victim - the deadly sigh of escaping gas!

Pentammonia Thional, Brains had called it - a super-coolant designed to operate Thunderbird 3's temperature control system. A gas to be handled with care, for its effect, though not fatal, would send a man to sleep for hours. And now it was escaping, spurt by spurt into the control cabin where John was sitting!

Odourless, colourless gas.

Minutes ticked by as the spaceship sped on its way towards Earth. When John Tracy felt his eyelids beginning to droop, he shook his head wonderingly, stood up in his seat and half-turned. Then he opened his mouth to speak, but only a croak came out, and he pitched sideways to the cabin floor.

Thunderbird 3 plunged on helplessly.

They were taking things easy at International Rescue headquarters. Brains, as usual, was deep in a scientific textbook, content to sit at the poolside and watch the others swim. Jeff Tracy sat beside him, listening to a transistor radio and glancing across from time to time, amazed that the scientist could shut out the music and the half-hourly urgency of the newscasts.

"Here is your twelve noon timecheck," said the radio, and at that, Brains looked up. "Gee! Is that the time already, Mr Tracy?"

"That's what the man said," replied Jeff smiling. "Why, Brains? Feeling like some lunch?"

"N-no, Mr Tracy. Er, but John should have checked in a routine course-change at eleven forty-five."

Jeff Tracy frowned. "Why, that's right Brains. Let's go see what kept him."

The two men walked into the innocent looking lounge, and Jeff pressed a hidden switch. At once, the inkstand on his desk tilted to reveal a microphone, and he selected John's call signal.

"International Rescue to Thunderbird 3. Come in, Thunderbird 3."

There was no answer. The portrait of John on the wall that should have clicked to a telescanner screen remained immobile.

"Something's wrong, Mr Tracy! I'll stand by the emergency link r-right away."

"Good grief!" Jeff Tracy was on his feet now, his knuckles white on the edge of the desk. "What's his course, Brains?"

"Th-that's just it, Mr Tracy. Something must have happened to him before he could make the change. The way he's going , he'll come through the atmosphere heading straight for New York, and his controls are set on manual. If Jodrell 6 wasn't dismantled for overhaul we could guide John in but there's nothing in the world we can do to stop him now!"

Still wet from the pool, Gordon, Scott and Virgil faced their father across the lounge. "We've got to do something, father!" It was Virgil who spoke. "There's got to be an answer!"

Jeff Tracy shook his head, his eyes screwed shut in desperate thought, his fists clenched. "But what? What? Think of a thousand impossible rescues, and our organisation can tackle them all - but this one..."

"Thunderbird 1 is the only thing fast enough to intercept, father," said Scott Tracy. "Let me take her up and see what I can do!"

"Er, it's not a spacecraft, Scott," broke in Brains. "whatever you attempt, it'll have to be within Earth's atmosphere."

"Whatever I attempt? Heck, is there anything I can attempt? But sitting here won't solve it."

His father nodded despairingly, and Scott made for the swivelling door that led to Thunderbird 1's entry system. "For Pete's sake think, think, think," he yelled as the door swung round. Keep the radio open all the time."

Within moments, the slender Thunderbird 1 was resting on its launch pad. Smoke and flame shot from its tail as it lifted off on its impossible mission.

"Changing to horizontal flight," said Scott "I'm beamed onto John's course. Estimated time of convergence, one hour."

A small video screen deep in the top-security building at New York, the home of the World Government's Central Attack Early Warning Control, glowed brightly.

On it, caught by ultra-range radio bounce, the image of Thunderbird 3, head-on, and homing fast.

General Omar K. Matheson straightened slowly, his jaw set in a hard line. The staff major at his side looked at him questioningly.

"It's one of the ships that the International Rescue uses," muttered the general. "Get on the link right away and find out what they're playing at."

The major did as he was told, and hurried back faster than he'd ever moved before.

"It's a runaway, sir! They claim to have an interceptor in flight now, but they report there's no definite plan of diversion!"

"No definite plan?" The general's eyes blazed, and points of red stood out on his cheeks. "Let me talk to them!"

Seconds later, General Matheson was speaking directly to Alan Tracy in the space satellite. He didn't mince his words.

"You listen here, feller. There are millions of people in this city, and if your ship takes its dive here, it's gonna be like a cartload of big-time bombs going off."

"It's in hand, general!" Alan tried to sound reassuring, but he knew as well as Scott that the chances of doing anything were slim.

"It had better be in hand," spat the general. "I'm alerting missiles, you get that? I'm giving your ship a ceiling boundary of four miles and the moment it comes in closer - pow!"

"You can't do that, general! There's a helpless man aboard Thunderbird 3!"

The general was unimpressed. "There are millions of helpless people in New York. One man's life against a million, which way would you jump, buddy?"

At the controls of Thunderbird 1, Scott Tracy took General Matheson's ultimatum with gritted teeth. Supposing he failed? He'd have a grandstand view to watch his own brother blown to bits.

Scott forced himself to push those thoughts to the back of his mind. He spoke coolly into the radio. "One hundred and fifty-two thousand feet, and still climbing. Before I can do a thing I'll have to get even higher."

Suddenly, he gave an excited yell. "I can see it! I can see Thunderbird 3!"

There it was, a distant speck against the vast sky, hurtling downwards like some crazy comet.

Now Brains came over the air, speaking urgently. "Remember, Scott, she's still on manual control. That m-means John will not have retracted the flight vanes."

"I follow, Brains. So they'll slow her down a little. But won't they burn off?"

The scientist stuttered a protest. "N-no! The metal I used is utterly resistant."

"Then I'm going to get as high as I possibly can, make a hairpin turn, and follow her down," said Scott. "I only hope this ship'll take it."

CONTINUED ON PAGE 44

GORDEIN TRACY

Gordon is the astronaut in charg of Thunderbird 4. At twenty-two-years of age he is the great joker of the Tracy fami and often has to be rebuked by his father. Adventure is Gordon's life and he revels in all water sports from skin diving to water skiing. In the Submarine Service and Worlc Aquanaut Security Patrol, he became an expert on oceanography and developed unique underwater breathing apparatus which he later modified and improved for International Rescue.

During his term of service with the WASP he commanded a deep-sea bathyscaphe and spent a whole year beneath the ocean investigating marine farming methods. Gordon is one of the world's fastest freestyle swimmers and is a past Olympic champion at the butterfly stroke.

Shortly after International Rescue began operating, Gordon was involved in a hydrofoil speedboat crash when his vessel capsized at 400 knots.

The craft was completely shattered and Gordon spent four months in a hospital bed. This accident served to control his exuberance and it taught him respect for the sea - an essential ingredient for anyone who pits his wits against the elements.

Date of birth: February 14th   Sash and trim colour: Orange

THUNDERBIRD 4

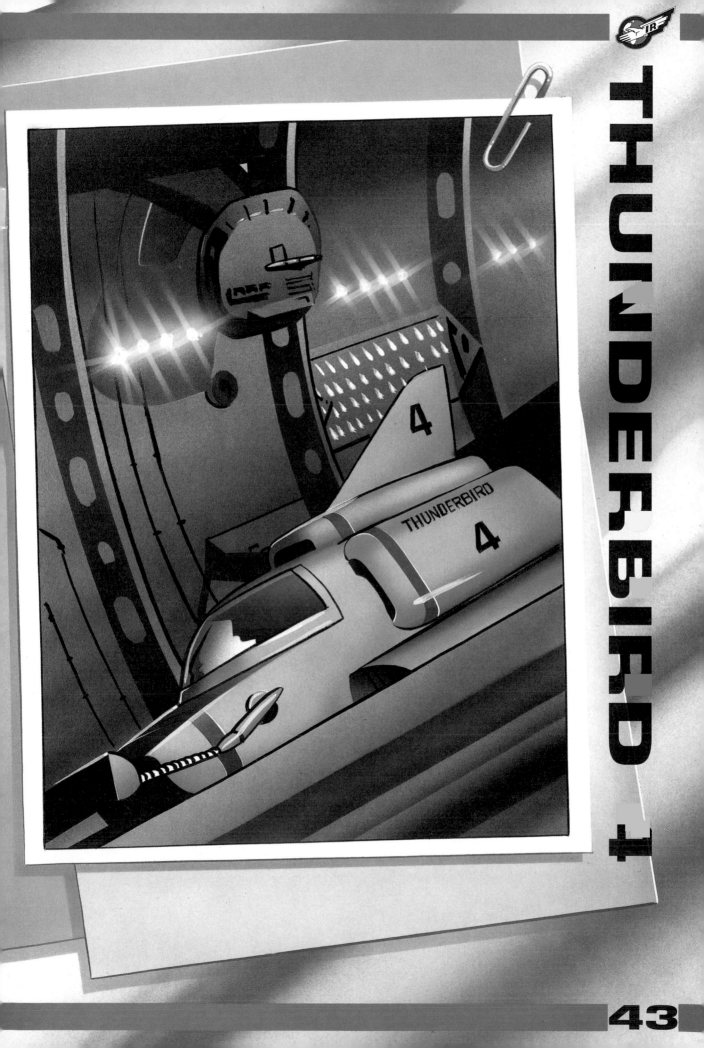

On converging courses, the two Thunderbirds were much closer now and Scott could make out every detail of Thunderbird 3 as he flung his own craft into a tight turn that threatened to black him out. He heard his own voice repeating: "I must hold on! I must hold on!"

Now the huge, blasting bulk of Thunderbird 3 passed him, dwarfing her sister ship so that Scott groaned aloud. "What can I do? What can I do? I can't get beneath her and carry her off, she's too big!"

There was silence from the radio. In the headquarters lounge, Jeff exchanged hopeless glances with the others. This was what they had feared all along - what they'd known, though they wouldn't admit it until the crunch came.

Scott was behind Thunderbird 3, and the craft was tossed like a toy in the backwash of the spaceship's rockets.

And then it came! The sudden flash of inspiration that might work. The mad ridiculous plan that only a fool or a desperate man would try!

"I'm going to shoot out her motors," Scott yelled into the radio.

Brains was quick off the mark. "Stop, Scott! It wouldn't do any good! You m-must realise the impetus of Thunderbird 3 would carry her onto the target regardless."

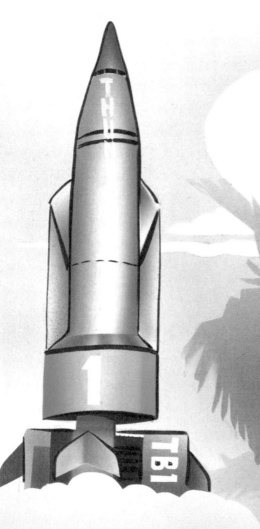

"Just a minute, Brains," shouted Scott. "You don't know the rest of it yet."

Carefully, Scott sighted the emergency missile carried in Thunderbird 1 and placed his thumb on the firing button. If he missed, it could be the end of his brother.

He held his breath and jabbed, and the missile streaked away to slam unerringly into the main motors of the runaway spaceship. At once the slipstream buffeting stopped and Scott relaxed his hands on the controls of Thunderbird 1. "Part one of the plan successful," he yelled. "Now for the real works."

"What the heck are you up to?" Jeff Tracy's voice crackled over the radio. But Scott didn't answer. His scheme was too far-out, too million-to-one.

Deliberately, he increased the speed of his ship and pointed the sharp nose straight for the dead motors of Thunderbird 3. His hand slammed down on the full boost lever, and instantly, he curled forward in his seat, his hands protecting his head, as Thunderbird 1 launched itself to collision!

The shattering impact flung him head-over-heels, across the control panel, against the screen, back over and under his seat, but miraculously he was unhurt. There was too much at stake to pass out now.

The nose of Thunderbird 1 had struck and lodged, buried deep within the shattered motors of Thunderbird 3. Now the two ships, a single united vehicle, sped on the same course downwards.

"I've done it! I've done it!" Scott couldn't help practically crowing the news to base. "If only Thunderbird 1's strong enough to steer the spaceship, we're saved."

Again there was silence from the radio, but this time, it was for a different reason. Messages were coming through rapidly on the land link, and they were coming through from General Omar K. Matheson.

"You'd better steer hard, and steer fast, Scott." Jeff's voice was as edgy as ice. "You're approaching the four mile limit Matheson set and he's not going to give way an inch. If you can't swing yourselves wide, those missiles are going to be on their way."

Scott hardly dared answer. Sweat stood out on his brow as he wrestled with his controls. Controls that suddenly wouldn't respond.

"It - it doesn't seem to have worked out, father," he groaned. "The spaceship's just too big. I can't get any movement at all."

"Stay with it, son! Stay with it!" Now Jeff's voice was harsh. "Keep trying - somehow you've got to move Thunderbird 3 or it will be curtains for you both."

Suddenly the tips of Scott's clenched fingers transmitted tiny vibrations up through his taut forearms, up through his straining muscles.

"Hey! We're shifting...by golly, we're shifting!" Slowly, but surely, the combined bulk of the two ships began to respond. Gradually, painfully, the image of the American continent below began to swing round on its axis.

And then, far beyond, Scott saw twin trails, like white pencil lines, drifting up towards him and his blood froze. "Father!" His hands were suddenly clammy on the controls. "New York have fired their missiles!"

Deadly, nuclear-tipped little rockets, sped upwards on their course of destruction, two needles of death launched by reluctant men, heavy hearted men...but men of determination. Above them, their target lurched and staggered across the sky, piloted by an equally determined man.

"It's like trying to steer a car with four wheels all of different sizes, and one of them square," said Scott into the radio. He'd read somewhere that men grow flippant, that they make jokes when they're staring death in the eye. Now he knew it was true. The missiles had become things of detached interest, to be watched, studied. Perhaps he'd try and read the code letters on their warheads in the moment before they struck home.

And then he realised they wouldn't strike home. The courses were so different. He could tell they'd miss by a mile. So odd, but he almost felt disappointed.

Scott shook himself out of his strange mood and watched the twin trails climb past him and go streaking out towards space. Then he looked below and saw the sea, and a fleeting glimpse of the west coast of America. So that was the Pacific Ocean.

Like a man in a dream, and tired like a man who should be in a dream, he called base.

"International Rescue from Thunderbird 1. You'd better get Virgil to bring out Thunderbird 2, selecting Pod 4. You'll need equipment for marine recovery and marine rescue, 'cos me and John, we're going down in the sea and we're going down very soon."

Fluttering from side to side like a stricken bird, the bonded mass of the two rescue vehicles kicked spray from the surface of the Pacific, bounced half-a-dozen times like a skimmed stone, and sank in ten fathoms off Moratoa Atoll.

The pool at International Rescue's island headquarters was full, as usual. There was an impromptu game of water-polo going on, and Scott, Virgil and Gordon were playing Tin Tin, Brains and John. John was fully recovered. Only Brains complained of trouble. "How c-can I see the ball without my glasses, fellers?"

And then Jeff Tracy came out to the poolside, and his grinning face made them all swim in and listen. Could it be a call for help?

"We've had a special request," said Jeff, "from a general who shall be nameless. It seems there are a couple of very expensive missiles orbiting around uselessly in space, with their jets burnt out and he wants to know if we'd consider going out to bring 'em back!"

Fair and handsome, twenty-five-year-old John is the dreamer of the Tracy household. Much of his time is spent as monitor in Thunderbird 5, International Rescue's space station, and in this position he is generally the first person to alert the island base of any disaster.

An electronics expert with a degree in laser communications, John is the quietest and most intellectual of all the boys. His favourite pastime is studying astronomy and his job as space monitor gives him ample opportunity to pursue this hobby.

The discovery of the Tracy quasar system was due to John's incessant space searching.

Although slight in build, John is a tremendously lithe and graceful person. At school he obtained many awards for athletics which he insists has contributed to his clearness of thought and mental agility.

Following in his father's footsteps, John became an astronaut after leaving Harvard University. This experience was invaluable when he returned home to become involved in International Rescue, for when Alan Tracy relieves him in the space station, the command of Thunderbird 3 is handed over to John.

Date of birth: October 28th   Sash and trim colour: Lilac

JOHN TRACY

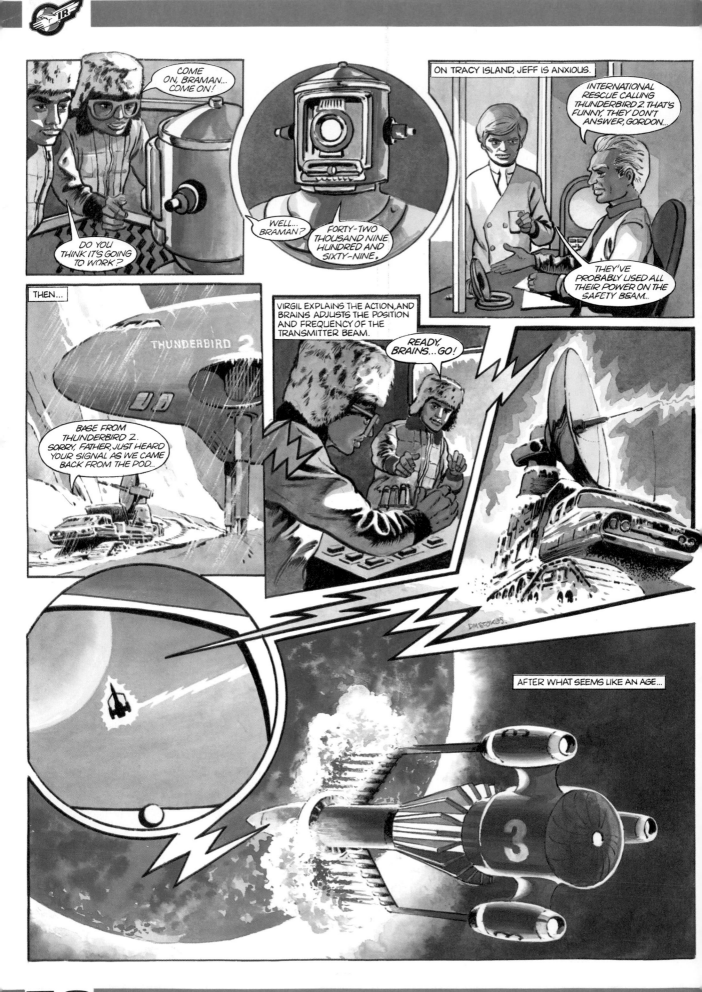

LADY PENELOPE

The London agent for International Rescue, Lady Penelope Creighton-Ward operates from her stately home in England.

Her ladyship's tastes in fashion are as modern as the designer's first pencil strokes. She has nerves of steel and quickly becomes bored with inactivity, choosing instead, to travel the world in search of adventure.

Gadgets of all descriptions are essential to Lady Penelope's role as special agent, and if she can discover a machine to complete the simplest of tasks she will install it in her mansion or pink Rolls Royce without a second thought.

The association between Lady Penelope and Jeff Tracy began when Jeff, having set up the International Rescue organisation, was looking for an agent in Europe. Penelope was already active as a brilliant spy and after a very difficult test, which she passed with flying colours, Jeff invited her to join the team. Since becoming a member of the organisation, Lady Penelope has proved her worth as valuable agent.

Date of birth: December 24th   Age: It is impolite to reveal a lady's age!

FAB 1

54

When Lady Penelope - International Rescue's London agent - wanted an assistant and helper, she knew the candidate would have to possess special talents.

Her ladyship's assignments required someone with the ability to move just outside the law, for safes and locks needed to be opened. After a long search, Penelope found the character who fitted the bill exactly.

He was reputed to be the finest safe-breaker in the world, he was known to be loyal to a fault and he was an excellent mechanic. His name was Aloysius Parker - sometimes referred to as 'Nosey' or 'The Nose'.

The approach was made, and after a few hours of gentle talking, her ladyship's charm bamboozled Parker into lifelong obedience and devotion to her every wish.

Even the long hours of social education which he had to endure did not upset Parker's respect for his new employer and teacher, but those long hours did very little to smooth the rough and ready edges of his personality.

Date of birth: May 30th Age: He says he's 52

THUNDERBIRDS
INTERNATIONAL
RESCUE
FAB
JETT
SCOTT
VIRGIL
ALAN
GORDON
JOHN
TIN-TIN

KYRANO
PENELOPE
PARKER
THE HOOD
TRACY
THE MOLE
FIREFLASH
SUNPROBE
CRABLOGGER
BRAINS

```
X H G F I R E F L A S H V A I
A Z F O M B Q S N I A R B G N
W E C P R Y C D O W B L V T T
J R B E E D C U C M O T F H E
C O E G X N O A R E U C S E R
R X B A S K E N R H T Y R M N
A O O I V Y F L S T J Q Z O A
B K R O I R P D O L T H N L T
L M P L R A O C N P H M K E I
O D N P G N S Q J A E R I K O
G S U H I D G F T R H J O H N
G G S T L Z A I F K O U V U A
E W N I Y L X C K E O J B D L
R I L Z A P A N P R D Y B A N
T H U N D E R B I R D S J T F
```

HIDDEN IN THIS GRID ARE THE WORDS LISTED ABOVE. HOW MANY CAN YOU FIND?

WORDGAME

The faithful friend and manservant of Jeff Tracy, Kyrano is of Malaysian extraction.

He has known his master for many years and there is nothing he would not do for the Tracy household.

Kindly and intelligent, he is an expert botanist and spent a number of years at Kew Gardens, England, advising on Asian species of orchids.

Jeff Tracy first met Kyrano at the Kennedy Space Centre. The inoffensive man was installed there to help produce synthetic food from plants. It was part of a programme to produce concentrated food in tablet and paste form to be used by astronauts in space.

Dealing with food helped Kyrano to

become interested in culinary arts, and after his scientific work at Cape Kennedy, he moved to Paris to become head chef in the Paris Hilton Hotel.

Kyrano's father was an extremely wealthy man, owning vast estates and rubber plantations in the East.

Instead of inheriting his rightful share in his father's will, Kyrano was deposed by his vicious half-brother and eventually lost interest in material gain.

He returned to Malaysia to a quiet semi-retirement, devoting his time to the education of his daughter Tin Tin. It was here that Kyrano, in strange circumstances, renewed his acquaintance with Jeff Tracy, after Jeff had suffered a nervous breakdown.

Later, when Jeff set up International Rescue, Kyrano did not hesitate to join his old friend, agreeing to run the Tracy household.

The arch villain of the world, the Hood is so named because of his many disguises. He is half-brother to Kyrano and wields an uncanny, supernatural power over Jeff Tracy's faithful manservant which he uses to his own advantage.

Unlike his brother, the Hood is gigantic in stature and has an evil face. His main aim in life is to acquire wealth to the exclusion of all justice

KYRANO

the Ho

nd right.
The largest target for his evil ambitions is International Rescue, for with plans of the organisation's machines he could auction the wonder-craft details to the highest bidder.

Operating from a strange temple deep within the Malaysian jungle, the Hood has eluded capture by stealth and infamous blackmail on characters who he suspects may betray him. Generally he works alone, but on occasions finds it necessary to employ criminals and the dregs of society.

Never can these unfortunate people get the better of their temporary master, for the Hood has a complete disregard for anyone but himself.

This makes him ruthless and calculating and his mystical powers hold him aloft as the world's most dangerous man.

Date of birth: July 17th   Age: 47

Aged twenty-two, Tin Tin, which in Malaysian means 'sweet', is the daughter of Kyrano. She was educated in America and Europe, with Jeff Tracy funding many of the expenses. He did this as a measure of repayment for her father's help during a difficult period, and for his faithful service.

Tin Tin was invited to join International Rescue after completing her studies in Europe, and she became involved in the organisation's first actual rescue operation when the Fireflash aircraft on which she was travelling was discovered to have a nuclear bomb aboard.

Her educational degrees in higher mathematics and advanced technical theory and engineering assured Tin Tin of a regular job with the International Rescue team. Her knowledge fits in closely with that of the organisation's engineer, Brains, who calls upon her for assistance in laboratory experiments.

Constantly checking and organising the maintenance of all the Thunderbird machines, she has repaid Jeff Tracy over and over for his generosity in financing her schooling.

Her main interests apart from her work include water-skiing, swimming and designing her own clothes...and Alan Tracy, who is constantly by her side.

Calling all
International
Rescue agents...
Jeff Tracy here.

We now have to close
this file on Thunder-
birds personnel and
activities and return
the data to the main
computer for secure
storage.

As special I-R agents, you
have established the right
to have revealed some of the
secrets of the Thunderbirds
organisation. But remember,
the details contained in
this bulletin are classified
for your eyes only.

ECRET £ I-R TOP SECRET £ I-R
F TRACY

Guard the secrets closely,
watch out for further
bulletins which will be
issued from time to time.

On behalf of my family
and all at International
Rescue, I thank you for
your attention.

Thunderbirds are go!

FAB

Signed

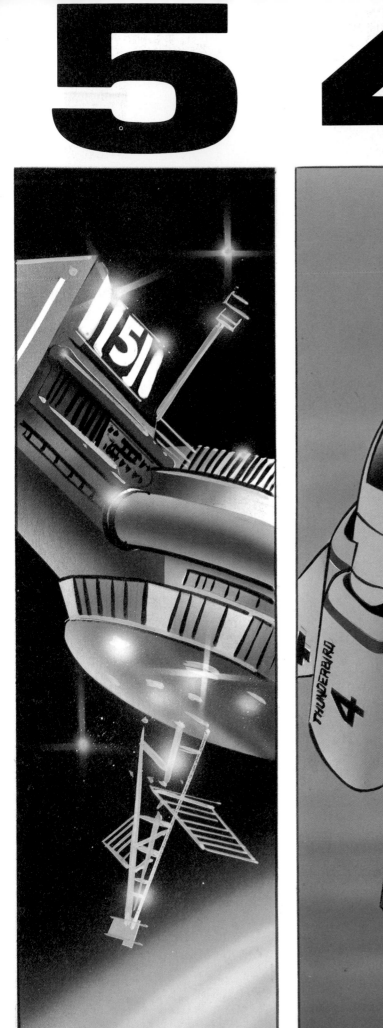
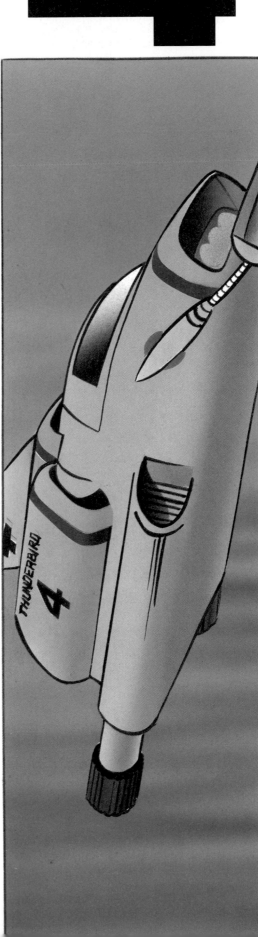

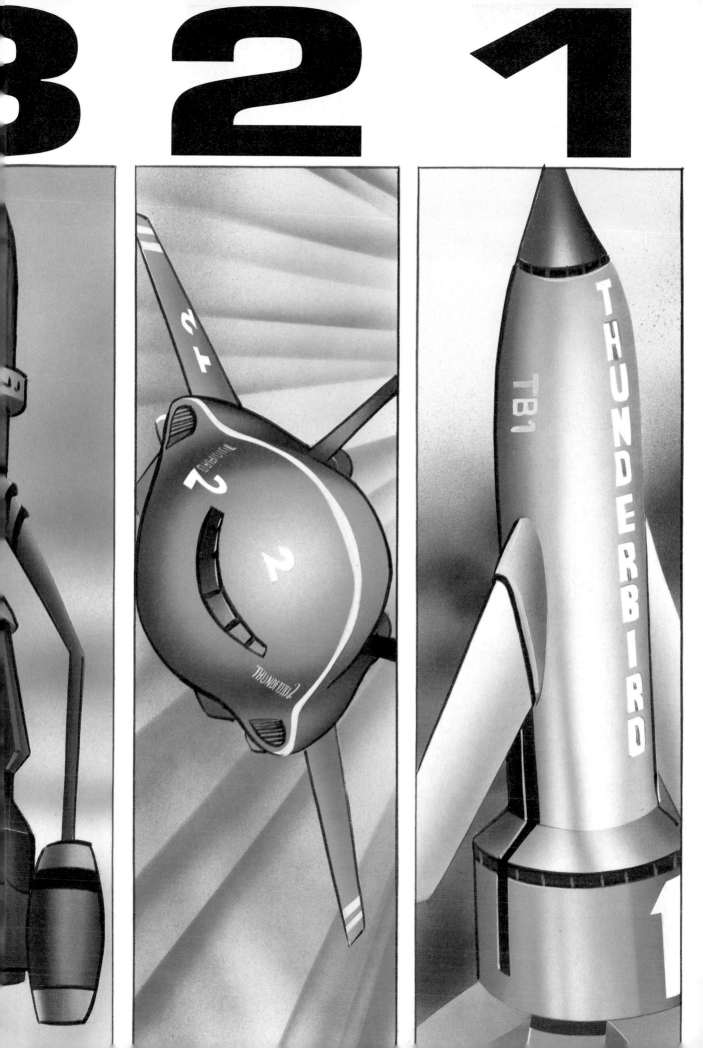